Confessions

AMY LAURENS

OTHER WORKS

CONFESSIONS

INKLET #44

AMY LAURENS

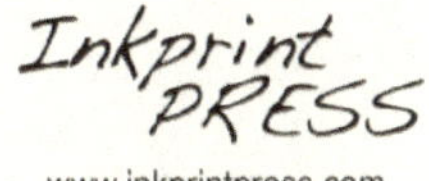

www.inkprintpress.com

Print ISBN: 978-1-925825-43-5
eBook ISBN: 9781393923602

www.inkprintpress.com

National Library of Australia Cataloguing-in-Publication Data
Laurens, Amy 1985 –
Confessions
38 p.
ISBN: 978-1-925825-43-5
Inkprint Press, Canberra, Australia
1. Young Adult Fiction—Fantasy—Dark Fantasy 2. Young
Adult Fiction—Art 3. Young Adult Fiction—Family—
Siblings 4. Young Adult Fiction—Short Stories

First Print Edition: October 2020
Cover image © Enrique Meseguer via Pixabay
Cover design © Inkprint Press
Interior art © Amy Laurens

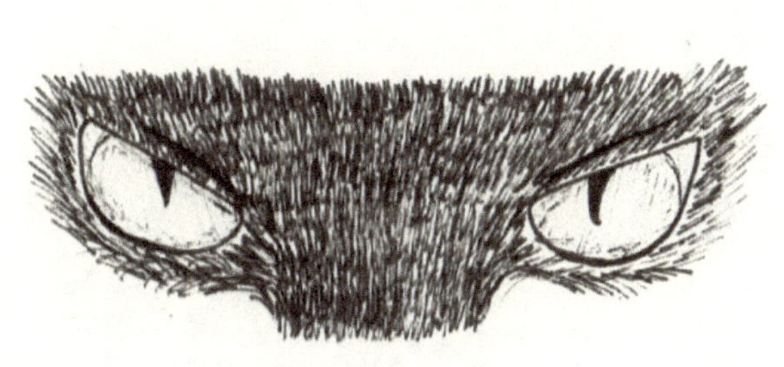

CONFESSIONS

T HERE'S A KNIFE ON THE TABLE, AND I don't know why. It makes me think that maybe they're going to sacrifice me after all, but jeans and a galaxy t-shirt don't really make for sacrificial clothes, so I don't know what's up with that.

I've been stuck in this room for five hours now—thank sanity they let me keep my watch, even though they took away my wallet, my phone, even my earrings and shoes—and I've no clue why they even brought me here.

At first I thought it was Tommy again—heaven knows they've hauled him in for questioning enough times, what with his 'extra-curricular activities'. But last time I saw him he assured me he'd given up the dope for good, and I believe him, and anyway if this was just about him they wouldn't have left me here to sweat for five hours alone with a ceremonial knife.

I have no freaking clue what they want me to do. I assume at some point they'll come question me, but half an hour ago I heard loud noises, explosions I think, and it's been silent ever since.

I want to know what's going on. Surely they won't mind if I just try the door, will they?

I ease myself up off my seat and inch towards the door. No doubt it'll be locked—it should be locked—why wouldn't it be locked?—if it's not locked I am going to be so mad at myself for not trying the door sooner.

Of course, it isn't locked. I'm an idiot. But not so much of an idiot that I leave the knife behind.

The creamy-sandy stone hallways are empty and silent. I'd expect that, in this part of the Council Chambers; the detention cells are hardly likely to be a bustling hub of activity, after all. But still. It's deathly quiet. Even the servers that should be whirring in the walls are silent.

I pad around a corner, the worn stone smooth and cool to my bare feet, and jerk to a stop, slapping a hand over my mouth to hold back a scream.

It's a body, blood-stained, dust-shrouded, in the uniform of a council guard. What could do this to a guard? They train for years to become the elite of the elite, and nothing can wipe them out, not even the mages.

Except.

Fear ripples through me, an icy cold hand on my shoulder and a plunging suddenness in my stomach. But it can't be true. And they wouldn't know, and they couldn't have brought me here for that.

I swallow, my throat suddenly dry and my hand clammy. If it is, I'm totally unprepared.

Unless they left a pencil lying around.

I move off and almost laugh at the stupidity of my own thoughts. Who leaves pencils lying around? Or pens, or even worse, permanent markers? The very thought sends ice and fire chasing each other down my limbs, first raw terror at the thought of such power, and second, longing for it.

The fingers of my free hand twitch, and I remember the feel of slender wood between them, the scruff-frrrrrt of graphite on thick, creamy paper. My throat is tight and it's hard to breathe. I close my eyes for a second, imagining a blank page, imagining control, imagining the images I need to bring my heart-rate down and flush away the adrenalin.

If I had some paper now, I could draw the most stupendous weapon, and then there'd be no need to fear.

But then there's another corner, and around it another dust-shrouded body, which sets the fear loose from the cage in my heart to run rampant around my lungs.

They can't know. They can't.

More corners. More bodies. The dust thickens so I can hardly breathe, and there shouldn't be dust here because this morning, five hours ago, I walked these passages and they were light and clean and full of people that bustled back and forth, going about their daily business with bright, sunny smiles and kind words.

But the dust. Only one thing could have caused so much dust.

Ahead I hear the snick-snick-snick of toenails on stone, and then a hoarse breath as though the dust itself could breathe. The trembling in my heart stills, though when I clasp the knife in both hands it slips, slick with fear-sweat.

My tongue sticks to the roof of my mouth and when I try to move it, I feel it tear.

My skin will tear worse than that if I cannot fix what I have done.

Deep breath, shoulders straight, stand tall. I will fix this, or I will die trying.

I round the final corner and stumble. In the middle of the Council Chamber's entry hall stands a monster, twelve feet tall and covered with bony studs the size of my fist but sharp, with a long tail like a herbivorous dinosaur might have had, and teeth like the bottom of the sea. But that's not what made me stumble.

Further on, behind the monster that I drew, lies one last body. It's small and frail, barely heavier than two baker's sacks of flour.

It's a body I know well, a body I love, a body I swore to protect.

I hear a strange sound, and realise it's the sound of my anguish, grief slipping out between gritted teeth for the sake of my broken baby brother. Fifteen is far too young for anyone to die.

My monster sees me, roars, and charges.

Hurriedly I swipe the tears from my eyes, gulp in the air, say my prayers. The knife is clenched between my hands, and I will die for what I have done.

As the monster looms over me, I have a bizarre moment of calm, and all I can think is that I should have been more careful with the perspective. He was only supposed to be one foot tall.

At least I was smart enough to draw a failsafe. Or not stupid enough to leave one out, whichever you'd rather.

The monster lunges at me, out-stretched claws as long as my fingers. I dive beneath them, score the knife along the bony plates, and trace out a symbol on its inner thigh. The monster reaches between its legs and rakes my back, shredding shirt and muscle and skin.

I scream. That was my favourite shirt.

Half laughing, half sobbing, I fight to keep the knife from wavering. If I can just finish the pattern, I'll find the place where the scales part, a tiny crevice just big enough for a knife—though it should have been a dinner knife, had the need ever arisen and I'd got the bloody perspective right.

It reaches for me again and my thigh

bursts open. Blood spurts and I scream and scream, but then the knife reaches the parting of the scales, and I stab it in as far as it will go. Not quite buried to the hilt, but it's the failsafe; it doesn't matter.

For a moment I think I've missed and the monster's still alive—but then it roars loud enough to burst my eardrums and I don't know whether to clap my hands over them as the memory of pain fades, or to slap at the blood pumping from my leg.

Either way, I'm going to die for my sins.

Charcoaled dust rains down on me, ashy, the dust that powdered the corpses, the dust from a pencil held greedily in unthinking hands.

I should have listened. A work of art is a confession. Best leave it to the priests.

THE MAKING OF *CONFESSIONS*

Urgh, the ending of this story. It kills me every time. Though not as much as our poor main character's sibling? ...Sorry. Trying to make light of a sad situation here. I usually can't cope with stories where children get injured, but apparently I wrote one?

Honestly, I'm not quite sure how this story happened. There was something on TV at one point about confessional art, and then there was something else on the internets about drawings coming to life, and the two collided, and here we are.

DOWNLOAD YOUR FREE EBOOK

When you buy a print book from Inkprint Press, we like to say THANK YOU by offering you the ebook for free!

Please head to www.inkprintpress.com/inklets/44/ and the use the coupon INK44 to get your copy of this Inklet in epub AND mobi today!
(Coupon will only work once.)

Read more by Amy Laurens!

A FOX OF STORMS AND STARLIGHT

CHAPTER ONE

S IX YEARS AGO, I SAVED A FOX IN THE bush. It was only because my dog died. At the time, it felt like a pretty crappy bargain.

It was the first day of autumn—not by the calendar, but by the fresh bite in the morning air, the golden quality of the light as it lit the main road through town in the mid afternoon.

Sailor was a big, black shaggy thing, something like a Newfoundland, a lively shadow in the golden light, and I was eleven.

I'm sorry to be starting any story this way, but the fact of the matter is, this where it all began.

I'll spare you the awful details. Enough to say that Sailor had got out of the yard somehow, and had been hit by a truck careening down the highway that split our tiny town in two as it blatantly ignored the speed limit.

I saw it happen.

And although I cradled him in my lap as the smell of burnt-out brakes and hot asphalt and turning leaves filled my nose, his giant, furry black head all of him I could fit, there was nothing I could do.

There was nothing anyone could do.

I knew that, but it didn't stop the knot of frustration and guilt in my chest, or the taste of bile in the back of my throat every time I closed my eyes and saw the truck hitting him, again and again and again.

It took years for that vision to fade.

But that evening, only a few hours after it had happened, everything still felt fresh, and raw.

Sunny, my sister, was only nine at the time. She cried for hours, just sobbing like she'd never breathe right again.

I'd cried a little, at the scene with Sailor's head lying in my lap as his big, brown eye stared up at nothing.

It had been mercifully fast, there was that.

And the driver had copped a massive fine—speeding, reckless driving, I think they even defected his truck—and came to visit us later, a big, pot-bellied man standing on our front verandah, shuffling his royal blue cap round and round and round in his hands as he apologised.

But that evening, with Sunny sobbing her heart out on the couch in the living room and Mum and Dad trying desperately to console her as dinner burned on the stove, I couldn't cry, even though the acrid scent of burning soy sauce, scorching brown sugar and smoking rice wine from the marinade prickled the back of my throat and the corners of my eyes.

I was the eldest, and I had to be responsible.

Possibly, if I'd been just a little more responsible, Sailor wouldn't have died.

So I slipped out the glass slider from the family room to the deck while Sunny cried, glancing up at the two storeys of our moody grey house behind me before jumping heavily down the three steps from the rail-less deck to the lawn, and set out for the gate in the back fence.

I couldn't cry, and I didn't want to add anything to an already chaotic and stressful situation inside—but I couldn't stay there, either.

In the gaps between the gum trees to the west, the sky tinged to red and gold at the horizon, the sun sinking slowly into oblivion. I'm pretty sure I didn't know the word oblivion back then, but I knew what it meant, how it felt—and I craved it, desperately.

Anything would be better than the gaping hole in my chest.

And so, because I didn't know where to find obilvion or how to get there, I stalked through the bush, pushing myself until I breathed hard and my lungs ached and sweat ringed me, chasing the way that hard exercise elevated me over my constantly looping thoughts.

Directly above, dark, heavy clouds obscured the sky, and the air was thick, heavy, humid.

Beneath the smell of dry gum leaves and even drier dirt, I could catch a hint of ozone, and occasionally the wind turned cool for a breath as it gusted against my skin, promising a late evening storm.

I walked harder, faster, outrunning the video looping in my mind of the truck's impact.

When the first drops of rain spat at me from out of the sky, I barely noticed. My skin was filmed with sweat, slick and salty, and the peppering of rainwater barely added to it.

That was at first.

But within minutes, it became clear that those first pattering spits had been the early foreshadowing of a storm darker and more intense than any I remembered.

Thunder rolled across the sky, distant and grumbling at first, a lazy background chorus to the rhythmic melody of the rain as it splattered down on grey-green leaves and red-tinged twigs, turning the silvered bark of an old, dead gum to deep grey and making the spiky, tussocky grass seem oddly luminescent in the dying light.

I stood under a grey gum with stains down its trunk that the rain was turning

orange, arms wrapped around myself, shi-
vering hard—and for the briefest instant,
thought about not going home.

Mum and Dad would pitch a fit.

And I had to be responsible.

I turned, dark t-shirt plastered to my
skin, dark hair sticking to my face and
clinging to my neck, and began trudging
my way back. The storm closed over prop-
erly, clouds rolling over the horizon and
cutting off the thin scythe of blood-
coloured sky, making the bush dark and
unwelcoming in the premature night.

Lightning flashed.

Thunder cracked hot on its heels.

I jumped—and stared hard at the gap
between two ghost-barked trees, where
for a second, I was sure I'd seen a pair of
eyes.

Nothing moved.

Nothing except the drenching rain,
anyway, weighing down the branches that
tossed fitfully in the wind.

The smell of wet dirt and soaked bark
rose around me, undercut by eucalypt and
ozone.

If anything had the power to wash away the hurt inside me, this storm was it. I tipped my face to the sky, imagining the rain washing over me had the ability to wash me inside as well, and the raindrops splattered hard on my face.

More lightning. More thunder, cracking over top of the constant hiss of the falling rain.

And in the distance, something eerie, lifting the hairs on the back of my neck: a strange kind of high-pitched howl, a cry that rang with moonlight and distance, cutting straight through the noise of the storm.

Bolts of lightning streaked across the sky—one—two—three in the space of half a second, followed immediately by a growling crack of thunder so immense it vibrated in my chest. I ducked instinctively.

There, in the corner of my eye…

I froze, crouched with my arms over my head.

The strange cries came again—and they were closer.

I stared hard at the place, low to the ground, where I was sure I'd seen something small, maybe the size of a cat.

Flash. Growl.

Rain spitting down.

There. Right there. A small animal, pointy ears, light coloured chin and throat…

The strange, eerie cries came a third time, and my heart pounded fiercely. Whatever was making the noise, it was close. Really close.

The little creature across from me reacted too, flattening itself to the ground.

My jaw twitched.

My heart pounded.

My fingertips bit into my upper arms.

Stay? Go?

Run? Freeze?

The hairs on my neck prickled again and goosebumps broke out all over me.

Cold dread formed a knot in my stomach.

Something was coming.

Something worse than the storm.

I had to get home.

I made it halfway to standing—and a series of strange, awful noises made me freeze again. They were sharp, clacking, squealing sounds, like someone knocking two echoing stones against each other, interspersed with high-pitched yowling...

And the creature in the darkness screamed.

I threw my back against the gumtree behind me, pressing hard against it. My heart hammered.

I peered back and forth in the dark, eyes wide.

Rain drenched down, but my throat was dry.

My pulse pounded faster.

The little creature screamed again—and as lightning flashed, I saw it on its back, legs slashing wildly at the air as something attacked.

The awful, clicking-yowling noises grew louder.

I slapped my hands over my ears, gasping. Water ran down my face, getting into my mouth, my eyes.

It was hurting.

Whatever the small thing was, it was getting hurt, and I'd seen enough animals hurting today.

Something in my chest snapped.

I flung myself across the ground, leaping a couple of tussocks and a fallen branch before I crashed to my knees.

I crawled closer, desperate, gasping for air through the heavy curtains of rain.

I couldn't see it. Where?

Somewhere here, near the base of that tree…

The yowling screeched right next to my ear. I cowered against the ground, spiky grass pricking my face, wet-earth smell smothering me—but now, there was a strange mustiness too, a cousin to wet-dog smell.

At the next flash of lightning, I saw it.

The creature was a fox—and something barely visible was attacking it, only the gleam of eye or flicker of teeth visible in the gloom.

But the damage was real enough.

The little fox's side had been opened right up, and in the bright, stark flashes of heavenly electricity, the blood was dark, thinned by the constant rain.

No.

No more animals were going to die today.

Not when this time, I could do something about it.

I snatched at a branch on the ground that turned out to be more of a twig, and launched myself toward the creature.

I had no idea what was attacking it, but I screamed and waved my handful of twiggy leaves anyway, batting them in the air over the fox like I knew what I was doing.

The horrible clacking cries ceased.

With one long, low rumble, the rain began to ebb.

Still gasping for air, pulse galloping in my throat, I sat next to the fox and shifted it carefully into my lap, realising as I tasted salt that I was crying.

I huddled over, trying to shelter the poor creature from the slackening rain, running my fingers over its wiry cheek— over and over and over and over.

"Please," I sobbed, throat tight and aching, chest constricted. "Please. Please don't die. Please."

Another gust of cool air washed over the clearing, taking the last of the rain with it—and lifting the goosebumps on my arms again.

I shivered, drawing the fox close, like it was a stuffed animal I could hug for comfort—its or mine, I couldn't say.

"Please. Please don't die. Please."

Something shifted in my lap.

Around us, the world stilled, dazed from the storm, but also something more, something watching, something waiting, as the bush held its collective breath.

The only sound was the occasional drip of rainwater from the gum leaves onto a fallen log—no insects, no wind, no rustling of leaves. Just… stillness.

And the fox, who shivered in my lap.

The clouds tore open, revealing a ragged triangle of stars that glittered in the fox's eye as it blinked open and stared up at me.

My chest snagged.

My throat ached from crying, and a headache was forming in the back of my head. But the fox blinked up at me—alive.

I ran a finger down it again, from nose to cheek to ear to shoulder, all the way down its side to its thick, bushy tail—and the wound in its side began to close.

Laboriously, it hauled itself to its front legs.

I tried to stop it—"No, it's okay, you can stay here, I'll look after you"—but it lifted its top lip to show half-hearted teeth, and staggered away.

As it did, I thought perhaps its fur began to shrink. And suddenly, it looked larger in the night—as large as a dog, as large as Sailor…

But I blinked, and it was just a trick of the light, because the creature that darted away into the bushes like nothing was wrong at all was clearly a fox, the size of a large cat or maybe a small beagle, and nothing more.

And if something screamed in the night not long afterward, and the cry sounded horribly, horribly human?

Well. I was halfway back toward home again by then, and I pressed my fingertips to my lower eyelids and prayed my parents wouldn't murder me for getting home so late.

Keep reading! Head to www.amylaurens.com/books/storm-foxes/ to buy your copy now!

ABOUT THE AUTHOR

AMY LAURENS is an Australian author of fantasy fiction for all ages. She loved drawing in high school, but it was a hobby that fell by the wayside as an adult. She's really enjoyed drawing for the Inklet series (but is glad none of the pictures have thus far come to life!).

Amy has also written the portal-fantasy *Sanctuary* series about Edge, a 13-year-old girl forced to move to a small country town because of witness protection, the humorous fantasy *Kaditeos* series, following newly graduated Evil Overlord Mercury as she attempts to acquire a castle, the young adult *Storm Foxes* series about magic and mental health, and a whole host of non-fiction.

INKLETS

Collect them all! Released on the 1st and 15th of each month.

INKLET #031
Welcome to Dark Dale
LIANA BROOKS

INKLET #032
When War Came to Town
A Powers Story
AMY LAURENS

INKLET #033
Not Fantasy
AMY LAURENS

INKLET #034
Courting the Winter Prince
LIANA BROOKS

INKLET #035
At the Home of the Winter King
A Storm Foxes Story
AMY LAURENS

INKLET #036
With This Ring
AMY LAURENS

DOUBLE ISSUE
INKLET #037
Venus &
Seven Reasons I Said No
LIANA BROOKS

INKLET #038
Oath Keeper
AMY LAURENS

INKLET #039
Forget
A Powers Story
AMY LAURENS

INKLET #040
NOT QUITE
Cinderella
LIANA BROOKS

INKLET #041
ONE BAD MAN
AMY LAURENS

DOUBLE ISSUE
INKLET #042
The Claustrophobia
Of Loneliness &
Adam, Be A Star
AMY LAURENS

INKLET #043
The Artist
as a Young Girl
LIANA BROOKS

INKLET #044
CONFESSIONS
AMY LAURENS

INKLET #045
But For Snow
A Kaitexos Story
AMY LAURENS

INKLET #046
The Boy
Named NO
LIANA BROOKS

INKLET #047
Anamata
AMY LAURENS

INKLET #048
A Wolf FOR
Christmas
AMY LAURENS